An Odd Job for Bob and Benny

NICK WARBURTON

Illustrated by Wendy Smith

Oxford University Press

Oxford University Press, Great Clarendon Street, Oxford OX2 6DP

Oxford New York
Athens Auckland Bangkok Bogota Bombay
Buenos Aires Calcutta Cape Town Dar es Salaam
Delhi Florence Hong Kong Istanbul Karachi
Kuala Lumpur Madras Madrid Melbourne
Mexico City Nairobi Paris Singapore
Taipei Tokyo Toronto

and associated companies in
Berlin Ibadan

Oxford is a trade mark of Oxford University Press

Printed in Hong Kong

Illustrations by Wendy Smith c/o Vanessa Hamilton Books Ltd.

Photograph of Nick Warburton © Eaden Lilley Photography,
Cambridge

A very odd job

Bob and Benny were out on their lawn painting a sign. Benny splashed on the colours and his brother Bob painted the words. It was a messy business, but they didn't mind mess.

When the paint was all gone, there was
the sign, finished. It said:

BENNY AND BOB: ANY ODD JOBS

BOB AND BENNY: ODD JOBS ANY

'That's us,' Bob said. 'We're going to be
odd job men, starting today.'

They fixed the sign to their front gate.
Then Benny went back to clean up the
lawn, and Bob went into the kitchen to
wash their jumpers.

That was when Mrs Catkin came along and saw their sign. She lived in the big house at the top of the village. It looked very grand, but inside it was rather ramshackle. This was because of Daisy, Mrs Catkin's pet elephant. Daisy was only a baby, but she was rather a lively baby.

Mrs Catkin wanted to visit her sister, but she couldn't take an elephant with her.

And she couldn't find anyone in the
village to look after Daisy. They all said an
elephant was too big and too *tricky*.

She looked over the fence and saw
Benny trying to wash the lawn.

'I've got an odd job for you,' she said. 'I
must go to see my sister and I want you to
look after my baby elephant.'

Benny was thrilled.

'Hooray!' he sang out, and skipped
round in a little circle.

That's why he only heard half of what Mrs Catkin told him. He heard her say 'sister' and he heard her say 'look after' and he heard her say 'baby'. The rest he missed.

'She can stay in your shed,' said Mrs Catkin, 'and she likes a bun now and then. And you will be *nice* to her, won't you, Benny?'

'Of course!' said Benny, bouncing up and down.

'Good. I'll bring her round tomorrow.'

Mrs Catkin went home and Benny rushed in to tell Bob the good news. Bob was thrilled, too. He and Benny danced round the kitchen, and bubbles and foam flew all over the place. It was a messy dance, but they didn't mind mess.

'But what is this job?' asked Bob, stopping suddenly.

Benny screwed up his eyes and thought hard. What was it Mrs Catkin had told him?

'I know,' he said at last. 'We have to look after Mrs Catkin's baby sister. She can stay in our bed and she likes the sun.'

'Are you sure?'

'Almost certainly,' said Benny.

'Then let's get ready,' said Bob.

Their own bed didn't look soft enough for Mrs Catkin's baby sister, so they found some cushions and piled them on top.

'She should be happy on that,' said Bob when they'd finished.

'She should be very happy on that,' said Benny.

Daisy

When Benny and Bob opened the door
next morning, they staggered back in
surprise at what they saw. Mrs Catkin
smiled and held out a note.

'I've put the instructions in this note,'
she said.

But Bob was too shocked to answer her.

'Benny,' he whispered, 'there's an
elephant on our doorstep.'

Benny could see that. He screwed up his
eyes and tried to remember what Mrs
Catkin had said to him yesterday.

'I think this must be Mrs Catkin's baby
sister,' he whispered back.

'It *can't* be. It's an elephant.'

'This is Daisy,' said Mrs Catkin. 'And
she's looking forward to staying with you.'

She gave Daisy a pat, put the note on
the mat, and turned to walk away.

Bob and Benny were too stunned to say goodbye. They stared at Daisy with their mouths open.

'Benny,' said Bob, 'you're a clot.'

'It was your idea to do odd jobs,' said Benny. 'You're the clot.'

For some moments they stood on the step, trying to knock each other's hat off.

Daisy watched them with interest. When their row was over, Bob said they ought to bring her indoors.

'After all,' he said, 'she is our guest.'

So they squeezed her through the door and led her into the house. Daisy liked the look of it. It wasn't too tidy and there were lots of interesting things she could pick up with her trunk.

'This is your bed, Miss Catkin,' Benny said when they got to the bedroom.

Daisy liked the look of the bed, too. She picked up some of the cushions and flung them around.

Then she put a foot on the mattress to test it out. There was a twanging sound and the bed fell in.

'Are you sure she has to sleep in our bed?' said Bob.

'Yes,' said Benny. 'Bed and sun, that's what Mrs Catkin said. I think.'

'Well, there's no sun in here, so we must think of something else.'

Finding the sun

After a while Bob had a good idea.

'We must put the bed on the lawn,' he said. 'So it can get the sun.'

'Excellent,' said Benny.

Some ideas are simple to think of but hard to carry out. This was one of them.

Bob and Benny tried to lift the bed. One stood at the top and the other at the bottom. Bob and Benny heaved and heaved but it didn't move, not even a tiny bit.

'Maybe,' said Benny, 'we should ask
Daisy to get off.'

'For once you've thought of something
useful,' Bob said.

They talked to Daisy in soft, sweet voices
but she took no notice. She liked Bob and
Benny's bed. She was happy there. All she
needed was a bun to make it perfect.

'This is no good,' said Benny. 'We can't lift the bed with an elephant on it. You'll have to think of something else.'

So Bob scratched his head and tried to think of another idea.

'We can't get the bed into the garden,' he said, 'so what must we do?'

'Bring the garden to the bed,' said Benny.

'Clot. If we did that, where would the sun be?'

'Where it always is. Outside.'

'So what must we do?'

'Bring the sun inside.'

'Yes. Exactly.'

Benny was pleased to be right, but he didn't know how they were going to bring the sun into the bedroom.

'That's easy,' said Bob. 'We'll make a hole in the roof!'

On the roof

Bob and Benny went outside to fetch the ladder. Daisy stayed on the bed. She was quite comfortable but she missed them. They were kind to her and they made her laugh, in an elephant sort of way.

She looked out of the window and saw them struggling with the ladder. They tottered backwards and forwards, trying to lean it against the house.

Then she saw them climb the ladder, disappear on to the roof, and she was alone again. Alone and hungry. She looked around the bedroom. Not a bun in sight. The cushions looked a bit like buns but they were really too big and too dry.

I'll have to go and look for one, she thought.

So she got up and wandered through the house.

Meanwhile, Bob and Benny were at work on the roof. They had a hard time of it because it started to rain.

'This is no good,' said Benny. 'The sun's gone.'

'Never mind,' Bob said. 'We must carry on.'

They pulled some tiles off and hammered away at the plaster. It was messy work, but they didn't mind mess. When they'd made a good big hole, Bob sent Benny back down the ladder.

'See what it looks like from the bedroom,' he told him.

Down went Benny and minutes later he stood in the bedroom.

'There's plaster and puddles everywhere,' he called up to Bob.

'Never mind that. Can you see the sky?'

'Yes.'

'And can you see it from the bed?'
'Yes.'
'And does Daisy like it?'
'I don't know.'
'Why not?'
'Because she's not here.'
'WHAT?'

Bob was shocked. He slipped on the wet roof and fell through the hole, landing on the pile of cushions. He bounced lightly up and down until, little by little, he came to rest.

'That was lucky,' Benny said.

'It was NOT lucky,' said Bob. 'I just fell through the roof.'

'But you didn't land on Daisy, did you?'

Bob jumped up. Of course! He didn't land on Daisy because Daisy wasn't there.

'We have to find her,' he snapped.
'Quick, Benny! Get looking!'

Benny picked up some cushions and looked under them. He moved the clock and looked behind it.

'Not in here!' said Bob. 'We must search the whole house!'

They ran through every room in the house, calling for Daisy, but she was nowhere to be found.

Where is Daisy?

Then Benny saw the letter on the door-mat.

'Oh, look,' he said. 'She's left a note.'

'Don't be silly,' said Bob. 'She can't write. She's only a baby.'

'Well, someone's left a note.'

Bob picked it up and read it. It was the note Mrs Catkin had left.

'Dear Bob and Benny,

Don't forget: be nice to Daisy. She can sleep in your shed and she likes plenty of buns.'

'Shed and buns,' said Bob, shaking the note at Benny. 'Not bed and sun!'

'Well, I was nearly right,' said Benny.

'You clot! Why didn't you listen?'

'And why didn't you pick the note up? You're the clot!'

'Oh, no!' said Bob. 'Look! The front door's still open.'

'Perhaps she's popped out to the baker's,' said Benny. 'To get some buns.'

'Yes!' said Bob. 'Brilliant! Come on!'

Out they ran, and up the street to the baker's, calling Daisy's name as they went. And – thank goodness – there she was, safe and sound, picking buns off the baker's shelf with her trunk.

Bob and Benny danced with joy at the sight of her.

And Daisy did a much heavier dance at
the sight of the buns. The only one who
wasn't dancing was the baker.

'Look at it!' he shouted. 'Look at it! It's
shop-lifting!'

But he calmed down when Bob paid him
for the buns and they led Daisy out of his
shop.

They put the cushions in their shed and
Daisy went in after them. She fitted very
nicely, and, with the door open, she had a
good view of the garden.

In the afternoon the rain stopped and she watched Bob and Benny mow the lawn. Then they got her to walk up and down to make the lawn flat. Daisy enjoyed that. She liked to be useful. They gave her the grass clippings on a big dish with a bun on top, and she enjoyed that, too.

When Mrs Catkin came back from her sister's, she was delighted to see Daisy looking so well.

'You've done a very good job, boys,' she said, and she paid them well.

With the money they bought two large umbrellas. When the rain came back that night, they lay in bed with the umbrellas up. They dozed off to the sound of the rain pattering on the umbrellas. It was still a bit messy, but they didn't mind mess.

About the author

While I was teaching, I enjoyed drama and reading books aloud with children. This encouraged me to write and since then I have written a number of scripts for radio, stage and television and a round baker's dozen or so – that is, thirteen – children's books. Sad to say, I am not good at odd jobs of any kind. When I was thirteen I made a table at school, but it fell off the bus on the way home and one of its legs came off.

   I enjoy reading, almost anything to do with cricket, and cycling around Cambridge, where I live with my family.

Other Treetops books at Stages 10 and 11 include:

Purple Buttons by Angela Bull
The Great Spaghetti Suit by Alan MacDonald
Janey's Giants by Nick Warburton
Dangerous Trainers by Susan Gates
Hilda's Big Chance by John Coldwell

Also available in packs
Stage 10/11 pack B	0 19 916902 0
Stage 10/11 class pack B	0 19 916903 9